MY BEST BEDTIME BOOK

ELLA BAKER

GALLERY BOOKS

An Imprint of W. H. Smith Publishers Inc.
112 Madison Avenue
New York City 10016

ILLUSTRATED BY JOHN BLACKMAN

CONTENTS

King Rumbletum's New Bed

"It's time we had a new bed," said the queen to King Rumbletum. "This one is years old. It's lumpy."

"I like the lumps," said Rumbletum. "I'm used to them."

"But the mattress is so thin. You can feel the springs. It sags in the middle."

"I like it saggy," said Rumbletum.

"Well I don't," said the queen. "It's not a proper sort of bed for a king at all. A king should have a king-sized bed, with a thick mattress and swishy curtains he can close. That's what a king should have."

And that's what Rumbletum was given, because the

queen was very determined. The old bed was moved out to the courtyard, ready for the garbage man to take away, and the brand new king-sized bed, with pink curtains, was installed in the royal bedroom.

"I don't like it," sulked Rumbletum, turning his back and staring through the window at his old bed.

"Nonsense," said the queen. "It's a beautiful bed."

Just then, the gardener's children ran into the courtyard. "Hooray!" they shouted when they saw the bed. "An old bed! Let's bounce up and down on it!"

"Look at those children bouncing on our bed," said Rumbletum. "It's a good bed for bouncing on, that bed."

"No bouncing on the new one," said the queen firmly.

Soon, the gardener's children were called in for supper. When they had gone, Mortimer, the cook's old dog, came hobbling along. Rumbletum liked Mortimer. He let him sleep on his feet at night. Mortimer took one

look at the bed, then he jumped on and stretched out
with a sigh.

"Look at Mortimer," said Rumbletum. "He looks so
comfortable on our old bed."

"No dogs on the new one," said the queen briskly.
"It's much too nice. Come along, Rumbletum, it's bedtime. Time to try it out."

"It's like being in a tent," grumbled Rumbletum.
"These curtains don't let any air in."

"It **is** rather stuffy," admitted the queen.

"It's too hard," muttered Rumbletum.

"Actually, I think it's a little soft," said the queen.

"I miss the lumps," said Rumbletum.

"And I miss the bumps," confessed the queen. "This
bed is altogether too smooth."

And they both sat up and turned on the light.

"I prefer our old bed," said Rumbletum.

"Me too," said the queen.

Up they got, and padded across to the window. Outside, they saw the old bed, bathed in moonlight. Mortimer was still stretched out, snoring peacefully.

"Shall we?" said Rumbletum.

"Let's," nodded the queen.

Together, they tiptoed down the stairs, through the big doors and out into the courtyard. They jumped into bed and pulled up the covers.

"Ah! Lumps," said Rumbletum happily.

"Mmmm! Bumps," agreed the queen.

Then, with Mortimer curled comfortably between them, the king and queen went fast to sleep.

The next day, the old bed was taken back to the royal bedroom, and the new one was given to the gardener's children.

"Old friends are best," said Rumbletum to the queen.

And this time, she had to agree with him.

The Sky Playground

Billy was fed up. He wanted to go to the playground but it was raining.

"We'll go if the sun comes out," promised his dad. But the sun stayed hidden behind the clouds.

Billy went to his bedroom and stared sadly out of the window. Just then, a small cloud bumped up against the glass. It almost seemed to be asking to come in.

Billy opened the window. The little cloud puffed into his room and hovered before him. Billy gave it a pat. It felt just like a cotton ball. He hopped on and the cloud sailed back out through the window.

Higher and higher they flew, until they reached all the other clouds. Billy bounced from one to the other. It was much better than a trampoline!

Lots of umbrellas lay around. People must have lost

them on windy days. Billy opened one up. The wind caught it and gently lifted him. His legs swung from side to side. It was lovely.

Then Billy saw the rainbow. It arched above him, one end disappearing down through the clouds. He scrambled up it until he was sitting on the top. Then he pushed off!

What a slide! Down, down, faster and faster, through the clouds, through the rain, straight through his window and on to the carpet!

"Billy!" called his dad. "Have you seen the rainbow? I think the sun's coming out. Shall we go for a walk?"

"Yes," said Billy eagerly. And on the way, he told his dad all about the sky playground.

Granny Grigg's Scarf

Granny Grigg liked knitting. She knitted while she watched television, and she knitted when she listened to the radio. She knitted while she talked on the telephone, and she knitted while she waited for the kettle to boil. She even tried knitting in the bath once!

Everyone knew Granny Grigg liked knitting, and they brought her all their leftover bits of yarn.

"Ooo! Lovely," she would cry. "That'll make a sweater for one of my grandchildren."

Granny Grigg's family did very well for knitted things. They all had hundreds of sweaters, scarves, gloves, hats and mittens. None of them ever caught cold, even on the most icy winter days.

One day, Granny Grigg was turning out her cupboard when she came across a huge bag of yarn. She had forgotten all about it. There were lots of tiny balls, all in different colors. "I'll make a scarf," she decided. "A rainbow-colored scarf."

She fetched her needles and began right away. She knitted all day, and all evening. She was enjoying herself so much, she took the knitting to bed. But soon she felt rather tired. So she put the light out, and it wasn't long before she was asleep. But, do you know, her fingers went right on knitting! Click, click, click, went the needles in the dark.

"Good gracious!" cried Granny Grigg when she woke up the next morning. "I've been sleep knitting! This must be the longest scarf in the world!"

It was. It started at her knitting needles, snaked across the room and vanished through the window! When Granny Grigg looked, she could see the other end dangling just above the flower bed.

13

"Enough is enough," she thought, and she cast off the stitches. Then she hauled the scarf back up through the window, and arranged it in neat coils on top of her bed. It nearly reached to the ceiling!

"I **am** silly," thought Granny Grigg. "Who would want a scarf that long? I wish I knew a giant." But she didn't. She would have to unpick the scarf.

"Oh well," she sighed. "I'll do it later. I'd better do my shopping first, before it starts snowing."

Outside, it was very cold. Granny Grigg shivered in the bitter wind. She was just stepping through the front gate, when she stopped with a gasp. She rubbed her spectacles to make sure she wasn't imagining things. But she wasn't. A man was walking up the road with a giraffe on a lead! The giraffe looked very unhappy.

"That giraffe looks frozen," Granny Grigg scolded the man. "Whatever are you doing, taking him for a walk on a day like this?"

"He's just come off the boat from Africa," explained the man. "I'm taking him to the zoo. I expect he does feel

a bit chilly. Africa's a hot country, and he's not used to the weather here."

"Wait right there!" ordered Granny Grigg. She had just had a wonderful idea.

She ran inside, and when she came out she was holding the scarf.

"It's perfect," said the man, and he climbed up a lamppost in order to wind the scarf around the giraffe's neck.

"It suits him," said Granny Grigg.

The giraffe thought it did too.

15

The Lullaby Lady

Have you heard of the Wakey Wakey Man? He's the mischievous clown who dances through the streets at night banging his drum. When children hear him, they sit up, wide awake, and leave their beds. They dance and play all night, under the Wakey Wakey Man's spell.

The Wakey Wakey Man's sister is the Lullaby Lady. She's not a bit like him. The Lullaby Lady is quiet and gentle. She wears a gray gown, and stars sparkle in her hair. When she sings, her voice is a mixture of water and laughter, wind and bird song. Even the Wakey Wakey Man has to listen, and like everybody else, is soon fast asleep.

Close your eyes. If you're lucky, you might hear her.

Katy Creeps
by Candlelight

Every night, Katy creeps up the stairs with her bedtime candle. Her shadow climbs with her to keep her company.

She reaches the top, and opens the door of her cold attic room. She places the candle on the old wooden chest, then runs across the bare boards to her bed. In she jumps, wriggling her frozen toes and pulling the blankets up to her chin.

The candle flickers. It's the only warm spot in the room. Soon, her grandma will creep in and snuff it out.

Katy doesn't mind. Through the window, the night blazes with one thousand candles. Katy thinks the Man in the Moon put them there, to light his way to bed.

She could be right.

Bradley Bear's Quiet Day

It was Sunday morning, early. Bradley Bear opened one eye. "Ah, good. Sunday," he thought. "I fancy a nice, quiet day," and he shut his eye again, so that it matched the other one.

"Oh yes?" sneered Popsy the cat. "He'll be lucky. Sunday morning is music morning for cats."

First, she scraped her claws down the window pane. Then, she rattled the cat flap to and fro. Next, she played drums on the cat food cans. Finally, she began to sing. "MEEEEEAAAAAOOOOOOOO!"

"Bother that cat," thought Bradley. "Oh well. I'll go outside and watch the insects."

Over by the plant pots, a butterfly warmed its wings in the sun. A snail crept from under a leaf and peered about. A ladybird slid down a twig with a gentle plop. Everything was quiet and peaceful.

Then . . . BANG! SMASH! THUMP!

Along came Jimmy, playing his garbage can lid. "Hi, Bradley! Look at my drum!" he shouted. "I'm going to play it all morning."

"You can if you like," thought Bradley. "I'm going fishing. Fishing's a nice, quiet thing to do."

Down by the pond, all was still. Bradley dangled his net in the water. "I hope I don't catch one," he thought, closing his eyes contentedly. "Too much trouble."

Then . . . RATTLE- JINGLE- CLATTER- PLONK!

Jimmy's sister, Jenny, came racing around the corner with lots of tin cans tied to her scooter. "Listen to my cans, Bradley!" she bellowed, screeching to a halt. "Don't they make a great noise?"

"No," thought Bradley, "they don't. Oh dear. **Now** where can I go to get some peace?"

In the flower bed, the flowers were growing so quietly, you could hear a petal drop.

"At last," thought Bradley, wriggling among them and staring up at the sky. "I shall stay here all day, smelling the flowers and watching the bees."

Then . . .

"Hey, Bradley! Listen to our band!"

There they were, all three of them. Jimmy was playing his garbage can lid, Jenny was rattling her cans and Popsy was singing. What a racket!

"Don't you want to join in?" asked Jenny. "You can play your trumpet."

With a huge sigh, Bradley turned and walked away.

"What's the matter with Bradley?" said Jenny, disappointed.

"Perhaps he just wants a quiet day," said Jimmy.

"Never mind. We'll play without him."

Bradley sat behind a bush, listening. It sounded as if Jenny and Jimmy were having a good time. In fact, they seemed to have forgotten all about him. He began to feel rather left out and lonely.

"That's enough of being quiet for one day," he thought. "I'll go and join in." And back he went.

In the yard, everything was quiet. Jimmy's garbage can lid lay on the ground. Bradley picked it up.

"Not now, Bradley," said Jimmy. "I'm reading."

Bradley picked up Jenny's tin cans and gave them a little rattle.

"Sssh," whispered Jenny. "I'm watching a little beetle. You'll scare it away. Can't you be quiet for a while? After all, it **is** Sunday."

"Huh," thought Bradley, and went off to play his trumpet on his own.

The Yellow Plastic Battleship

"Come along, Rumbletum," shouted the queen. "Your bath's ready."

"Goody," said Rumbletum, who enjoyed his bath. "Here I come!"

In he came, wearing his pink bathrobe, matching slippers and crown. He paused, frowning down at the bubbles. "Hold on," he said. "Where's my yellow plastic battleship?"

"I'm sure it's in there somewhere," said the queen carelessly.

"No it isn't," said Rumbletum, poking around among the floating toys. "The rubber octopus is here, and the diver. And there's my sailing boat, and the three ducks, and the wind-up shark and the swimming Mickey

22

Mouse and my pouring pelican and my squirting squid. But where's my yellow plastic battleship?''

"Does it matter?" said the queen. "You've got quite enough to play with. In you get."

"No," said Rumbletum. "Not without my battleship." Which was very silly, but then, Rumbletum was silly sometimes.

With a sigh, the queen ordered the servants to search the palace. They found all kinds of things: lost balls and odd socks and apple cores and candy wrappers, but they didn't find the yellow plastic battleship.

The hunt went on for a whole week. The palace garden was searched, the moat was drained and notices were put up in the town.

But the battleship remained missing.

All this time, Rumbletum refused to have his bath. He sat sulking in the coal shed, his favorite sulking spot, still wearing his bath robe, slippers and crown.

LOST
ONE YELLOW PLASTIC BATTLESHIP — REWARD GIVEN TO FINDER

"Don't be so silly, Rumbletum," scolded the queen. "Look at you. You're filthy."

"I don't care," said Rumbletum stubbornly. "I want my battleship."

The queen didn't think he deserved one after all that fuss, but she was so tired of him, she went to the toy store and bought a replacement.

"This isn't right," said Rumbletum when she gave it to him. "It's red. My old one was yellow."

"Oh, go and get it yourself then," cried the queen.

So Rumbletum came out of the coal shed and went to the toy store, just as he was, in his dirty pink bathrobe, grubby slippers and crown.

"A yellow plastic battleship, please," he said to the storekeeper.

"Go away," said the storekeeper. "We don't serve dirty people."

"But I'm the King!" shouted Rumbletum.

"Ha, ha," laughed the toy store man. "A likely story. Whoever saw a king as dirty as you?"

"I've got a crown," argued Rumbletum, pointing.

"Obviously fake," said the toy store man. "Go on. Clear off."

So Rumbletum had to go home, because the toy store man wouldn't serve him.

"It serves you right," said the queen. "And by the way, here's your silly old battleship. I found it in the dog basket. It's all chewed up."

"Oh dear," said Rumbletum. "I remember now. I swopped it for Mortimer's rubber bone. I'm sorry, dearest."

"So you should be," snapped the queen. "Get in the bath immediately."

And, humbly, Rumbletum did.

It was freezing!

Wicked Wayne

Wicked Wayne was a very naughty boy. He ran up the DOWN escalator, and he ran down the UP one. He went in through doors marked EXIT, and he went out through doors marked ENTRANCE. He screamed for candies. He wouldn't share his toys.

"Oh," cried his parents. "What shall we do? What shall we do with Wayne? We tell him NO, but then he goes and does the same again!"

They took him to the principal. Wayne made rude faces.

"He's too wicked for me," said the principal. "Try the doctor."

"Oh," cried Wayne's parents to the doctor. "What shall we do? What shall we do with Wayne? We tell him NO, but then he goes and does the same again!"

Wayne blew down the doctor's stethoscope.

"He's too wicked for me," said the doctor. "Ask a policeman."

"Oh," cried Wayne's parents to the policeman. "What shall we do? What shall we do with Wayne? We tell him NO, but then he goes and does the same again!"

Wayne broke the policeman's pencil!

"He's too wicked for me," said the policeman. "Try the zoo."

"Oh," cried Wayne's parents to the zoo keeper. "What shall we do? What shall we do with Wayne? We tell him NO, but then he goes and does the same again!"

"Leave him to me," said the zoo keeper. "I'll put him in with the monkeys."

Everyone laughed when they saw Wayne in the monkey cage.

"Let me out," he shouted. "I'll be good." And he was.

Fred's Holiday

Fred Flake was a snowman, and he fancied a holiday. He lived in a cold country, you see, and was beginning to get rather bored with all the snow.

The other snowmen thought Fred was mad. "There's nothing wrong with snow," they said. "Snow's lovely."

"Well, I'm bored with it," said Fred. "I'm going to book a holiday somewhere warm. I want to sunbathe. I'm going to the Bahamas where it's hot."

"You'll be sorry!" laughed the other snowmen.

But Fred was determined. He went right ahead and reserved himself a first class seat in the refrigerator of an airplane which was going to the Bahamas.

"Help yourself to ice cubes, Mr Flake," said the air hostess, shutting the door.

"This is great," thought Fred. "A window seat would have been nicer though."

When Fred reached the Bahamas, he went straight to the beach. "So this is a beach," he thought. "It's wonderful. That blue stuff must be the sea. Now. How do I sunbathe?"

He looked around at all the sunbathers. "I see," said Fred. "I have to buy some sunglasses and a towel." So he bought sunglasses and a towel, and lay down.

Five minutes later, Fred felt a little warm.

Ten minutes later, he felt uncomfortably hot.

Fifteen minutes later, he felt distinctly **runny**.

"Help!" said Fred. "I'm melting. Help!"

Luckily, the beach was full of children, and children like snowmen. They particularly liked Fred, because he was the only snowman in the whole of the Bahamas, which made him rather special.

"Quick!" yelled a small boy. "Fred's melting. Hurry up everyone. Bring your buckets!"

All the children ran up with their buckets, and scooped up Fred. By now, he was more water than Fred, and rather mixed up with sand. But the children made sure they had all of him, then they ran as fast as they could to the ice cream parlor.

"There's been an accident," they told the ice cream man. "The sun was too hot, and Fred Flake's unfrozen! We've got him in our buckets. Can you help?"

"Certainly," said the ice cream man. "I'll pop him in the freezer for a bit. Then I'll rebuild him. Don't worry, he'll be as good as new."

So he did. And Fred was. And what's more, the ice cream man liked him so much that he offered him a job in the ice cream parlor.

Everyday, when the children came along, they would bang on the side of the freezer, and shout, "Three vanilla cones, please!" And Fred would pop up.

Fred had a wonderful holiday. In fact, he liked living in the freezer so much, that he decided to stay forever. "There's nothing wrong with being a snowman in the Bahamas," he would tell the surprised customers, "as long as you don't sunbathe."

Gordon's Trip

Once, a lonely little goldfish lived in a bowl. His name was Gordon. The bowl had nothing in it except water and Gordon. All he ever did was swim around and around and hope somebody would remember to feed him.

"This is dull," thought Gordon. "I wish I could swim in a straight line." But he couldn't.

One day, he was swimming around as usual when a giant hand loomed above him and dropped a strange object into the bowl.

Splash!

Gordon was terribly excited. Nobody ever dropped anything into his bowl except food, and that wasn't very often. He swam down to examine the object. It was pale pink, and had an opening at the front. When Gordon listened at the opening he could hear a swishing, roaring sound coming from deep inside.

"What a lovely noise," thought Gordon. "I'll find out what it is," and he swam into the opening.

He found himself swimming along a dark, curving tunnel with smooth sides. As he swam on, he could see a tiny spot of green light far in front of him. The spot grew bigger and bigger, and Gordon finally swam out into a beautiful world.

The water was warm and clear. Colorful fish darted about among rocks and swaying water weeds. "Come and join us!" they called in a friendly way.

"Hooray!" thought Gordon as he hurried off to join them. "At last I can swim in a straight line!"

You, too, can hear the sea when you press a sea shell to your ear. But you have to be as small as Gordon to get to it that way.

Goldilocks and the Three Bears

(Traditional tale)

Once upon a time, there were three bears who lived in a little house in a wood. Father Bear was the biggest. He had a big chair, a big bowl for his porridge, and a huge bed. Mother Bear had a middle-sized chair, a middle-sized bowl, and a middle-sized bed. Baby Bear had a small chair, a little bowl, and a tiny bed that fit him just right.

One morning, they made some porridge for breakfast. It was very hot, so they decided to go for a walk in the wood while it cooled.

While they were gone, a little girl called Goldilocks came to the house. She peeped through the open door and, as no one was there, she went in.

The lovely smell coming from the bowls of porridge made Goldilocks feel very hungry. First, she tasted Father Bear's porridge. It was too hot! Next, she tried Mother Bear's porridge. It was too cold! Then, she tried Baby Bear's. It was just right, so Goldilocks ate it all up.

Goldilocks decided to sit down. First, she tried Father Bear's chair. That was much too high. Next, she sat in Mother Bear's chair. That was too hard. Then, she sat in Baby Bear's chair. It was just right but Goldilocks wriggled so much that one of the legs came off!

Goldilocks felt rather tired, so she went into the bedroom. First, she climbed up on Father Bear's bed. It

was much too lumpy. Next, she lay down on Mother Bear's bed. That was too soft. Then she tried Baby Bear's tiny bed. It was just right, and soon she was fast asleep.

When the three hungry bears came home, Father Bear stared at his big bowl and said in a loud, gruff voice, "Who's been eating **my** porridge?"

Mother Bear looked at her bowl and said in her middle-sized voice, "Who's been eating **my** porridge?"

And Baby Bear looked at his bowl and said, in his tiny voice, "Who's been eating **my** porridge, and eaten it all up?"

Father Bear looked at his big chair. "Who's been sitting on **my** chair?" he grumbled loudly.

"Who's been sitting on **my** chair?" complained Mother Bear.

"Who's been sitting on **my** chair, and broken it?" squeaked Baby Bear.

Then the three bears went into the bedroom. "Who's been sleeping on **my** bed?" roared Father Bear.

"Who's been sleeping on **my** bed?" asked Mother Bear.

Baby Bear stared at his tiny bed. "Here she is!" he cried. "Here's the girl who ate my porridge and broke my chair!"

At that, Father Bear gave a loud, angry roar.

Goldilocks woke up at once. With a cry of fright, she rushed to the window and jumped out. She ran home as fast as she could, and her mother was very cross with her for wandering off on her own.

When Goldilocks had gone, Baby Bear helped Father Bear and Mother Bear mend his chair. Then they made some more porridge, and finally sat down to a big breakfast. And the next time they went for a walk, they made certain they locked the door!

Llamas in Pajamas

Yesterday, we went to the zoo. Sue liked the elephants. Ted preferred the snakes. Me? I liked the llamas. They've got such snooty expressions.

When I went to bed, I remembered I needed to buy new pajamas. That, and the zoo visit is probably why I had this strange dream.

I was in the desert, and there were some llamas walking towards me. The funny thing was, they were all wearing pajamas! I asked the leader why. She looked at me very snootily, and said: "It gets very cold in the desert at night. Llamas always wear pajamas. Fancy not knowing that."

I didn't, but I do now.

Spots and Stripes and Squiggly Lines

When I went to buy new pajamas, it was very confusing. There were so many different designs to choose from.

"Get spots," said Sue. "Big purple spots."

"Stripes," said my dad.

"Squiggly lines," said Ted. "Or battleships."

"The ones with big green squares are cute," said Mom.

"Zig zags," said Grandad.

"Flowers," said Grandma.

I couldn't decide. It was all too much for me. Finally, I went home and wore my old, faded blue ones. They're getting a bit tight now, but I'm fond of them.

If the store sold old, faded blue pajamas, I wouldn't have a problem. Perhaps I'll write and suggest it.

The Very Special Slippers

Old Toby the shoemaker was working late. He was putting the finishing touches to a very special pair of slippers. They were a birthday present for his young granddaughter, Nancy, who was going to be five the next day.

The tiny slippers were pale blue and lined with soft fur. Each had a silver bow on top. They were the most beautiful slippers that Toby had ever made.

Just as Toby sewed the last stitch and snipped the thread, there was a knock at the door. Toby placed the slippers on the bench, and went to answer it.

Outside, stood a fat man wearing a long fur coat. It was Maximilian Moneybags, the richest man in town. He lived in a big house on the hill with his daughter, Miranda.

"Good evening, shoemaker," said Maximilian Moneybags. "I have a slight problem. It's Miranda's birthday tomorrow, and all the stores are closed. I saw your light on, and wondered whether you have a pair of shoes I could buy for her. I must get her something, or she'll scream."

"Why, certainly, sir. Come in," said Toby. He pointed to a shelf of children's shoes. "There are some pretty red ones with buckles – or perhaps your daughter would prefer these yellow ones," he said.

But Maximilian Moneybags wasn't listening. "Aha," he said, picking up the very special slippers. "I need look no further. These are perfect."

"Oh no, sir," cried Toby. "Those are very special. They're for my granddaughter, Nancy."

"Nonsense. I shall pay you well."

"I'm sorry. They're not for sale," Toby said firmly.

"I see," said Maximilian Moneybags coldly. "Well, in that case, I suppose I'll have to take the red shoes. Do you have a box?"

"Of course," said Toby and he hobbled off to find one.

"Here you are, sir," he said, coming back into the room. But the room was empty. Maximilian Moneybags had gone, and so had the very special slippers! In their place were three silver coins.

The next day, Toby went to visit his granddaughter.

"Hello, grandad," called Nancy as Toby walked up the path. "Have you made me some birthday shoes?"

"I'm afraid not, Nancy," said Toby, and he told her what had happened. "These silver coins are for you," he finished up.

"Thank you, grandad," said Nancy. "But I'd rather have had my slippers."

Nancy tried to enjoy her birthday, but somehow it just wasn't the same without her grandad's present. "I'm so sorry about the slippers,'' she whispered when he came up to kiss her goodnight. "Were they **very** special? Tell me what they were like.''

"Blue,'' said Toby, "with a fur lining.''

"And silver bows,'' added Nancy.

"Why, yes. But how did you know?''

"Look,'' whispered Nancy, pointing out of the window.

Toby looked. Down the road, two tiny blue slippers came dancing, the street lights reflecting off the silver bows! They slipped through the bars of the gate, tripped up the path and sat quietly on the doorstep, waiting to come in.

"Oh, grandad!'' exclaimed Nancy. "They really **are** special, aren't they?''

"They certainly are,'' agreed Toby, shaking his head. "Let's go down and see if they fit.''

They did. Perfectly.

Slip, Trip, Slithery Bump

Barry Baboon lived in the jungle. He liked climbing trees, playing tricks and eating bananas.

One day, he picked a big bunch of bananas and scampered up a tall tree to eat them. He peeled the first one and carelessly threw away the skin. It landed at the bottom of the tree.

Soon, a tiger called Talbot walked by. He didn't notice the banana skin. Slip, trip, slithery bump! Talbot fell head over heels and landed painfully on his bottom.

Barry laughed and laughed.

"Just you wait, Barry!" shouted Talbot crossly, and he went off to find a cool pool to sit in.

"What fun," thought Barry. He ate another banana and threw down the skin.

Along came Bessie Boar. She was so busy looking for ground nuts, she didn't notice the skin. Slip, trip, slithery bump! Down fell Bessie, hurting her nose quite badly.

Barry laughed and laughed.

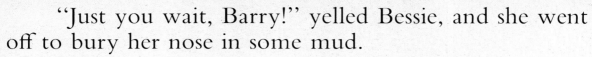

"Just you wait, Barry!" yelled Bessie, and she went off to bury her nose in some mud.

"Nobody can get me up here," thought Barry gleefully. He threw down yet another banana skin.

Along came an elephant called Earl. He put out his great big foot, and . . . . . slip, trip, slithery bump! Down sat Earl, very surprised.

Barry didn't laugh. He was too busy falling! You see, when elephants fall, the ground shakes. That makes the trees shake. Barry's tree shook so much, he couldn't hold on. Barry didn't slip, trip or slither, but he went bump all right!

Talbot, Bessie and Earl laughed and laughed.

King Rumbletum's Sleepless Night

King Rumbletum liked going to bed. It made a change from sitting on his throne all day.

One night, however, when the servants had put his crown away, breathed on his pajama buttons to warm them and finally tiptoed out, Rumbletum found that he just wasn't sleepy.

"Sleep well, dearest," said the queen, turning out the light.

But Rumbletum couldn't. He tossed and turned. He punched the pillows and threw them on the floor. He heaved and sighed. Then he sat up. "Dearest," he said. "I'm still awake. Are you?"

"Zzzzzzzzzzzzzzzz," said the queen.

So Rumbletum got up. Everyone was sleeping, so he had to amuse himself. First, he clanked around in a suit of armor. That was at midnight.

At one o'clock, he rollerskated down the corridors.

At two o'clock, he slid down the stairs on a tin tray.

At three o'clock, he played the trumpet.

At four o'clock, he tested the fire alarm.

At five o'clock, he played pool.

At six o'clock, everybody got up. They hadn't slept a wink with all that noise. That's when Rumbletum declared he felt sleepy, and went to bed!

The same happened the next night, and the next. Everyone was exhausted. Something would have to be done.

The musicians played him lullabies. Rumbletum danced wildly.

"New pajamas!" thought the queen. "That should do the trick," and she bought him some handsome black ones with yellow stripes. Rumbletum spent all night roaring through keyholes, pretending to be a tiger.

People brought milky drinks. Rumbletum poured them away.

A man came who told long, dull stories. He bored himself to sleep, but Rumbletum stayed wide awake.

Finally, they sent for the doctor.

"Boredom and laziness," said the doctor, "that's your trouble. I prescribe twenty-four hours sleep for everyone else, and a dose of hard work for you."

"What's hard work?" said Rumbletum.

"You'll see," said the doctor. "Off to bed, everyone. Rumbletum, you're going to look after yourself for a change. Get busy!" Then off he went, while the queen and the servants sank gratefully into their beds.

"What fun! I'll start with breakfast," thought Rumbletum. "I'll have scrambled eggs," and he went to the kitchen. That was at midnight.

At one o'clock, he scraped out fourteen burnt saucepans.

At two o'clock, he cleaned thirty broken eggs from the floor.

At three o'clock, he washed his socks.

At four o'clock, he hung them on the line.

At five o'clock, he watered the plants.

At six o'clock, he began ironing. That took all morning. Lunch was an apple. He didn't dare try cooking again.

The rest of the day was spent cleaning the palace from top to bottom. By seven o'clock, he was so tired he could hardly stagger up to bed.

"Dearest," said Rumbletum to the queen. "Hard work is very tiring. Did you know?"

"Zzzzzzzzzzzzzzzz," said the queen.

"I shall sleep forever," yawned Rumbletum, climbing into bed.

He didn't, of course. But, as he had discovered that hard work was tiring, everyone made sure he did some everyday, just as the doctor had ordered. And never again did Rumbletum find that he just wasn't sleepy.

Scruffy's New Clothes

Scruffy Scarecrow had a problem. His Aunt Fussy had invited him for lunch, and he didn't have a thing to wear. Aunt Fussy had been a dummy in a store window when she was young, and was particular about clothes. Scruffy always looked a mess, with his shabby old jacket and wild straw hair sticking out from a battered felt hat.

"I wish, just this once, I could turn up looking well dressed," he sighed to his friends the crows.

The crows liked Scruffy. He wasn't a bossy sort of scarecrow at all. "We'll see what we can do," they told him, and they flew off to think about it.

That morning, Farmer James was getting ready to go out. "Where's my best suit?" he said.

"Hanging by the window. It smells of mothballs," said Mrs. James.

"Well, it's not there now," said Farmer James. "I can't find my new hat either. And where's my best blue shirt with the matching tie? I laid them out on the bed, all ready to wear, and they've gone. In fact, all my best clothes have vanished! I've been robbed, mother! You shouldn't have left the window open."

"Don't be silly, dear," said Mrs. James. "That window's too small for anyone to climb in. Next, you'll be blaming the birds!"

At exactly that moment, the crows were admiring Scruffy. He looked very handsome indeed.

"Thanks everyone," said Scruffy, putting a flower in his buttonhole. Then he set off to Aunt Fussy's for lunch.

51

The House-Proud Robot

Mr. McTavish was an inventor. He had invented a garden hose but it sucked up all the plants, and he had invented a vacuum cleaner but it spat out dirt. He wasn't very good at inventing, but he enjoyed it.

One day, Mrs. McTavish sighed heavily. "Housework, housework!" she said to Mr. McTavish. "We waste so much time doing housework. I'm tired of it."

"Hmmm," said Mr. McTavish thoughtfully, then he vanished into his workshop. He stayed there for three weeks, only coming out for meals.

Then, one night, he opened the door. By his side stood a small metal box on legs.

"Meet Rex," he said proudly. "He's programed to

do all the housework. Right, Rex?"

"Right," said Rex in a tinny voice, "and I'll get started now."

And he did. He dusted, swept and polished. He washed curtains, cleaned windows and watered plants. He cleaned up cupboards and ironed clothes. At the end of the day, the house sparkled.

"Thank you, Rex," beamed Mrs. McTavish. "Have a rest now. I'll cook supper."

"And mess up my clean kitchen? Certainly not," said Rex. "I'll do it."

"Delicious supper," said Mr. McTavish. "Thank you, dear."

"Rex cooked it," said Mrs. McTavish. "He won't let me in the kitchen."

Rex came waddling in to collect the dirty dishes. "Tch, tch," he tutted. "Look at all these crumbs on the floor! Now, I want you both out from under my feet. I've lots to do this evening."

Mr. McTavish went outside to try to fix the hose.

Mrs. McTavish went to visit a friend.

"Wipe your feet!" ordered Rex, when Mr. McTavish came back in. "Don't drop your coat there," he scolded Mrs. McTavish as she came through the door. "Hang it up in a proper manner."

Mr. and Mrs. McTavish went to bed. Rex didn't, though. Rex shampooed the carpets. They could hear him shifting furniture about, and shouting at the cat for coming in with muddy paws.

"Er – dearest?" said Mrs. McTavish. "About Rex. Don't you think he's perhaps just a little too house-proud? I don't feel it's our own home any more."

"I'll fix him in the morning," promised Mr. McTavish.

The next morning, Mr. McTavish took Rex into his workshop and fixed him. "I think you'll find there's a difference," he told Mrs. McTavish.

There certainly was. Rex began to make a mess! First, he emptied the wastepaper basket all over the cat. Then he took a box of eggs from the refrigerator and dropped it on the floor!

"Ooops! I've adjusted him too much the other way," sighed Mr. McTavish, and he grabbed Rex and whisked him back into his workshop. The door closed, and Mrs. McTavish began to clean up with a sigh.

A little later, the door opened, and out came Rex. "I'm sorry about before," he said. "I think he's got me right now. I'll help you do that, Mrs. McTavish."

Together, Mr. and Mrs. McTavish and Rex cleared up the mess. And this time, much to everyone's relief, Mr. McTavish **had** got Rex just right. They all became firm friends, and the house was always clean and straight without being uncomfortable – which is just how a house should be.

A Teddy Bear Who Snores

It's hard to sleep in our house. It's just too noisy. Doors are always banging. The dog is always barking. My sister's always talking on the telephone. My brother practises on his drum kit, the cat asks for his food, the parrot asks for his bird seed.

My dad starts hammering the minute I go to bed. I don't know what my mom does in the kitchen — saucepan juggling, I think. I'm the only kid I know whose grandad sings loudly in the bath and whose grandma plays the trumpet. I've got sneezing uncles and coughing aunties. **But worst of all . . . . .**

MY TEDDY BEAR SNORES. No, really. I have a teddy bear who snores.

I've tried everything. I've stuffed him under my pillow. I've buried him under the bedclothes. I've put a clothespin on his nose. I'd put him in the cupboard, but I know he likes to sleep next to me.

ZZZZZZZZZZZZZZZ.

The trouble is, everyone thinks I'm making it up. Nobody else can hear him, for the simple reason that **they're all too busy making their own noise!**

But he snores all right.

Ted

Ted's the name of my teddy bear. He's a bit bald, with one eye missing, but of all my toys, I like him best. Bedtime wouldn't be the same if Ted wasn't there.

Sometimes, when I get cross, I'm horrid to Ted. I throw him around and shout at him. Once, I even pulled his ears, and they both came off in my hand!

I felt sorry right away. After all, Ted hadn't done anything.

I asked my mom to sew them back on again. Ted looked better, but I could tell from his expression that he was still a bit upset. So I bandaged him up and put him to bed. I brought him some grapes, just like I do when someone's in hospital. I could see he was enjoying the fuss.

The next day, he was back to his old self. He didn't say a word about the day before.

That's the nicest thing about Ted. He always forgives me real quick.

Sammy and the Sandman

It was bedtime, and Sammy's mother came to say goodnight.

"Go to sleep, Sammy," she said. "The Sandman will be here soon."

"Who's the Sandman?" asked Sammy curiously.

"He's the man who sprinkles star dust in your eyes to make you sleep well."

When his mother tiptoed out, Sammy lay awake thinking about the Sandman. "I wish I could see him," he thought.

Suddenly, there was a noise like the tinkling of faraway bells, and silvery light flooded the room. Sammy sat up and stared in wonder.

An old man with a long white beard stood before

him. His cloak glittered with tiny stars, and in his hand he held an empty sack.

"Oh dear," sighed the man. "Now I've done it. You're not supposed to see me."

"Are you the Sandman?" asked Sammy.

"Of course I am. Who do I look like, Santa Claus? I shouldn't be talking to you though. You're supposed to be asleep. The trouble is, I've run out of star dust. There's a hole in my sack, and the dust has been trickling out all evening. I'll have to go all the way back to the Moon to collect some more now, and lots of children won't be able to sleep tonight."

"Perhaps I can help," said Sammy eagerly. "You can collect the dust in my bucket. It's very good for sand. I'm sure it would be perfect for star dust."

"Well, thank you very much," said the Sandman. "It would save me a journey."

Sammy jumped out of bed and ran to his toy box. He handed his bucket to the Sandman.

"You're very kind," said the Sandman. "As you're
awake, perhaps you'd like to help me collect the star
dust?"

Sammy nodded excitedly.

"Hold my cloak, then, and take a deep breath."

Before Sammy knew what was happening, they had
risen into the air and were flying out of the window!

"There's some dust!" shouted the Sandman, pointing
down to the tall tree in Sammy's garden. "Let's start with
that!"

Down they swooped, landing on the very top
branch. Sammy gathered handfuls of the soft, cold silver
dust and put it carefully in the bucket.

"There's more on the roof over there," said the
Sandman. "Hold tight!"

Off they flew, landing lightly on the roof, where
they gathered more star dust. They flew from tree to tree

and rooftop to rooftop, until Sammy's bucket was full.

"That's enough," said the Sandman. "Thank you for helping me, Sammy. Now close your eyes."

And that's the last Sammy knew. When he awoke, it was morning and his mother was pulling back the curtains.

"Oh, Mum," said Sammy. "I've had such an adventure! Last night the Sandman came, and I helped him gather star dust."

"What a lovely dream," said his mother. "But why is your bucket on the windowsill? I wish you'd put your toys away."

Sammy knew the Sandman must have left it there. He scrambled out of bed, and ran to look. In the bottom of the bucket were a few silvery grains.

"Sand," said his mother.

"Star dust," whispered Sammy.

Ben's Boots

Ben had new red boots. "Can I go for a walk?" he asked his mom on the first rainy day.

"Certainly," said his mom. "Wear your new boots."

Ben put on his raincoat, his hat, and finally his new boots.

"Very handsome," said his mom. "Those should keep your feet dry."

Ben set off down the road. As he walked, the rain rained harder. It rained on all of him, but mostly it rained down his new boots.

A big, soaking wet dog bounded up. He stopped right next to Ben and shook himself. More water went in Ben's boots. His feet felt very damp, but he walked on.

Next, a car zoomed by. A great wave of dirty water splashed up, landing – guess where? In Ben's boots, that's where!

Ben squelched on down the hill. At the bottom, there was a huge, muddy puddle.

"I'll wade across," thought Ben. "It can't be that deep."

It was. Three steps, and the water was lapping around the top of his boots. One more step, and it poured in, filling his boots right to the top.

Ben looked down at his new red boots. Then he stooped and took them off. With one under each arm, he waded back through the puddle and walked home in his socks.

"I don't know why I bother to buy things," scolded his mom. "What do you think boots are for?"

"Not for keeping feet dry," said Ben, and he went to look for his slippers.

The Picnic in the Woods

It was a lovely hot day – just right for a picnic in the woods. Jimmy took his ball, Jenny took her jumping rope and Bradley Bear carried the picnic basket, because he was good like that.

"Let's go tree climbing!" suggested Jenny when they reached the woods. "Bradley, you guard the basket. We won't be long."

"I've heard that before," thought Bradley.

In the wood, two squirrels were playing follow-my-leader around the tree trunks.

"I'll play too," thought Bradley. "They won't mind."

The squirrels had never seen a bear before. They ran off as fast as they could. Bradley went after them, thinking they were playing. They ran under a bush. Bradley squeezed after them, and scratched his ear.

They ran along a fallen tree trunk. When Bradley tried it, he fell off and bumped his nose.

They jumped over a muddy ditch. Poor Bradley didn't see it in time, and fell in with a big plop. Falling with a plop hurts less than falling with a bump, but it's dirtier.

The squirrels ran up a tree and shook their tails at him.

"I give in," sighed Bradley. "It's hard work playing with squirrels. All that running and squeezing and falling and plopping is not for bears."

Suddenly, he remembered something. He was supposed to be guarding the picnic basket! He hurried

65

back – but oh dear. The worst had
happened. The picnic basket had gone!

"Thieves!" thought Bradley. "Thieves
have stolen the picnic! I must look for
clues and track them down."

First, he found a pile of crumbs.

"Cheeky things," thought Bradley.
"They've eaten a sandwich. I hope it
wasn't one of mine." Then he felt guilty.
After all, it was his fault the basket had
been stolen.

Further along, he found a piece of
orange peel.

"These thieves are very careless," he
thought, and he put the peel in his pocket,
as woods should be left neat and clean.

Next, he found an apple core.

"I'd better catch them," he thought,
"or there won't be any picnic left."

Then he heard voices.

"Bradley! Up here!"

Bradley looked up and there were Jimmy and Jenny, waving down at him from a tall tree.

"We came back for you, but you'd gone," shouted Jimmy. "Mind your head, the elevator is coming down."

"What elevator?" thought Bradley. Suddenly, the missing picnic basket was dangling before his nose! It was tied to the end of Jenny's jumping rope.

"We're having the picnic up here," called Jenny. "It's fun! Hop in, we'll haul you up!"

Bradley eyed the basket doubtfully. "Oh well," he thought. "I've scratched my ear, bumped my nose and landed in a muddy ditch. I might as well fall out of a basket." So in he jumped.

Within moments, he had been hauled up safely and had landed on a wide branch. The picnic was laid out, all ready to eat.

"You're very muddy, Bradley," said Jimmy. "Did you have fun without us?"

"No," thought Bradley, "I didn't." But when he ate his first sandwich, he felt much better. Picnicking up a tree was such fun, he couldn't stay miserable for long.

The Bed That Grew

Annamaria had a hot, milky drink in bed. "Drink up, Annamaria," her mom said.

"No," said Annamaria. "I don't want it."

"Nonsense," said her mom. "It'll make you grow big. When I come back, I want to see that mug **empty**."

"All right then," thought naughty Annamaria. "I'll empty it." And she did. All over the bed!

As soon as she had done it, she was sorry. She knew there would be **big** trouble. There was. The bed began to grow!

"What's happening?" cried Annamaria as her bed shot upward.

CRASH! It burst through the ceiling! Annamaria peered over the edge. The bed legs were growing taller and taller. She could see through the hole in the roof down into her bedroom, which was getting further away every second. Soon, she could see the whole town! "Stop!" she shouted.

But it didn't. Soon, it was so high, that the world looked just like a big beach ball.

That bed didn't stop growing until it was as high as the Moon. Luckily, the Man In The Moon was in, and able to help. "Shrinking powder is what you need," he said. "I'll sprinkle some on. Hold tight!"

Annamaria held tight and, to her relief, the bed began to shrink. Down, down, down, until at last she ended up in her own room. The hole in the ceiling mended itself just as her mom came in.

"Good girl," said her mom. "You've finished your drink I see. Now you'll grow big."

"I'm not sure I want to," said Annamaria.

The Three Little Pigs

(Traditional tale)

Once upon a time, there lived an old mother pig who had three little pigs called Tubby, Porky and Podge. One day, she called them together and said to them, "Children! You are growing too big to live in my small house. You must go and build your own houses to live in. But remember, be careful of the wicked wolf."

Off went Tubby, Porky and Podge.

Before long, Tubby met a man carrying some straw. "Please man!" said Tubby. "May I have some straw to build a house?"

"Certainly," said the man.

So Tubby took the straw and he built a house with it. He was very pleased with the house. But suddenly, he heard a voice. It was the wicked wolf. "Little pig! Let me come in!"

"No!" said Tubby, trembling. "Go away!"

"Then I'll huff, and I'll puff, and I'll blow your house in!" shouted the wolf, and he did. But he was too late. Tubby had escaped out of a window.

Meanwhile, as Porky was walking along, he met a man with some sticks. "Please, man!" said Porky. "May I have some sticks to build a house?"

"Certainly," said the man.

So Porky took the sticks and he built a house with them. But, just as he had moved in, he heard a voice.

It was the wicked wolf. "Little pig! Let me come in!"

"No," said Porky. "I won't."

"Then I'll huff, and I'll puff, and I'll blow your house in," roared the wolf, and he did. But he was too late. Porky had escaped out of a window.

Meanwhile, as Podge was walking along, he met a man with some bricks. "Please man!" said Podge. "May I have some bricks to build a house?"

"Certainly," said the man.

So Podge took the bricks and he built a house with them. It was a fine strong house, and Podge was very pleased with it. One day, when he had moved in, his two brothers ran to his door and he let them in. Then he heard the wicked wolf's voice: "Little Pig! Let me in!"

"No," said Podge, stoutly. "I won't."

"Then I'll huff, and I'll puff, and I'll blow your house in," bellowed the wolf. And he huffed, and he puffed, and he huffed again. But, try as he might, he couldn't blow down Podge's house.

The wolf was furious. As soon as he got his breath back, he climbed on to the roof and started to scramble down the chimney. But Podge was a clever pig. He had a big pot of soup boiling on a fire in the fireplace. He soon realized what the wolf was up to, so he took the lid off the pot.

When the wolf was half-way down the chimney, he saw the huge pot. With a startled yelp, he fell right down the chimney and into the pot, and that was the end of him. And Podge and his brothers lived safely and happily in the little brick house for ever after.

Where Moonflowers Grow

The old lady lived in a tumbledown cottage on the hill. The roof leaked, the windows were broken and the door flapped open when the wild winds blew.

"You can't stay here, you know," said Mr. Worthy from the Housing Department. "This house isn't fit to live in. We'll give you another one down in the town."

"No thank you," said the old lady. "I want to live where the moonflowers grow."

"I can't see any flowers," snapped Mr. Worthy, staring out into the overgrown garden. "But if you don't want to live in another house, you can move into a home for old people. Some have gardens."

"Do moonflowers grow there?" asked the old lady.

"I really have no idea," said Mr. Worthy. "You're being very difficult. We're going to have to pull this house down and that's that."

Mr. Worthy put on his coat and stepped outside, slamming the door behind him. He thought the old lady was quite mad, with her talk of moonflowers. As he started off down the garden path, the moon came out from behind a cloud and there was a rustling sound behind him.

Mr. Worthy turned, and it was then that he saw the moonflowers. Their petals were uncurling as the moon beams touched them and they glowed with a pale light. Tall and graceful, they were the most beautiful flowers he had ever seen.

Mr. Worthy went back and knocked on the old lady's door. "You can stay here," he said. "We'll repair your house. Of course you must stay where the moonflowers grow."

Green's Great

It all began at breakfast, when the green galumpetty monster said he wouldn't eat his green grass.

"Eat up, there's a good monster," coaxed his mother.

"NO," said the green galumpetty monster, who wasn't good. "I hate green food."

"Go to your den then," ordered his mother. "When you're sorry, you can come out and eat your greens."

So the green galumpetty monster went to his den. But he didn't stay there. He sneaked out the back way.

Outside, it was a bright shiny morning. Green galumpetty monsters were everywhere, nibbling the grass.

"Yuck," said the green galumpetty monster loudly. "I hate green food."

They all stared in amazement. "Green's great," they told him. "You're crazy."

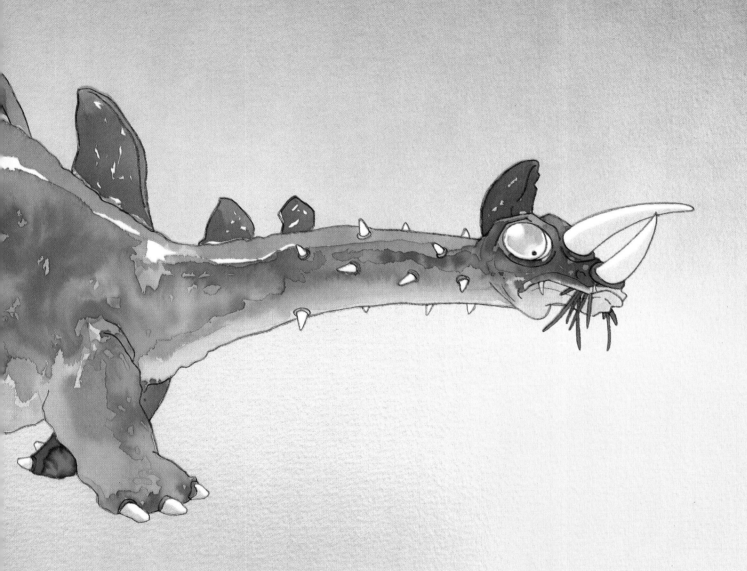

"Ha ha," smirked the green galumpetty monster. "That shocked them. Now to find some different-colored food!"

Further down the mountain, three humans were unpacking a picnic basket.

"It's a perfect day for a picnic," said the father. "I'm glad I thought of it."

"I've never been up Monster Mountain before," said the child. "I hope we see some monsters!"

"Ho ho! Silly child," laughed the mother. "Monsters don't exist."

"OH YES THEY DO," said a voice from the bushes, and out clumped the green galumpetty monster, wearing his very best friendly smile.

"Help!" screamed the father and mother.

"Hooray!" cheered the child. "It's all right, he's a friendly monster!"

But the father and mother didn't know he was friendly. All they saw was a howly scowly, grumpy growly monster rushing toward them. They raced off down the mountain, taking the child with them. The green galumpetty monster was sorry about that. He rather liked the child. Still, there was the picnic to think about.

The monster had never seen such wonderful food.

Yellow bananas, red tomatoes,
Pink iced cakes and blueberry pie.
Silver fishes, golden butter,
So many different things to try.
Purple plums and brown sliced bread,
Juicy oranges – what a spread!

There was green lettuce too, but the green galumpetty monster ignored that, of course.

He ate everything else though. Every last crumb. "Now," he thought. "I'll hurry home and sneak in the back way. I hope mother and father haven't missed me."

They had, of course. They were waiting for him. He knew he was in **big trouble** when he saw their faces.

"Oh no!" gasped his mother. "What's he been eating? Just look at him!"

The green galumpetty monster clumped to the mirror and stared. He hardly recognized himself. He wasn't green anymore. He was a multicolored monster, with yellow ears, pink paws, a blue body with golden spots, silver whiskers, brown legs, a purple tail, orange teeth and a bright red nose!

You see, if green galumpetty monsters are to stay green, they must eat green food. Regularly. The young monster had to eat bowl after bowl of good green grass before he turned green again. He didn't mind though. The different colored food hadn't tasted that nice anyway. "Green's great," he thought, "for green galumpetty monsters, anyway."

When Alligator Cleans His Teeth

When Alligator cleans his teeth,
It takes him quite a while.
For such an awful **lot** of teeth
Make up his wicked smile.

Twenty tubes of toothpaste –
And that's quite a lot of paste –
Will vanish down his throat each night
Because he likes the taste.

He wears out loads of brushes
And he's always buying more.
They tend to call him Sir, a lot,
Down at the toothbrush store.

Up and down and to and fro,
Over, then beneath,
That's the way that Alligator
Likes to brush his teeth.

And when he's finished brushing,
Though he still looks simply frightful,
His teeth look fine, and have a shine
That's really quite delightful.

Which Brush?

What color is your toothbrush? Mine's red. I always choose red, because it's my favorite. My dad's is yellow, and my mom's is blue. My sister, Sue, has a green one, and my brother, Ted's is white. We all know our own toothbrush, because of the color.

One day, my dad went to the store and brought back a box marked FIVE TOOTHBRUSHES – SPECIAL OFFER.

"They were very cheap," he said, opening the box.

Inside were five toothbrushes. One each. The trouble was, **they were all orange.**

"How will we know which is ours?" we all asked.

"I never thought of that," said Dad.

The Leaky Kettle

"I must replace this old kettle," said Mrs. Brand with a frown. "It's got a leak. Besides, it takes ages to boil. I shall buy a new one tomorrow." And she turned off the kitchen light, and went out.

In the kitchen, there was a shocked silence. At last, someone spoke. "Did you hear what she said?" hissed Freezer. "She's getting rid of Kettle!"

"It's a disgrace!" agreed Washing Machine.

"What shall I do without Kettle?" sniffed Teapot.

Food Mixer and Coffee Grinder tutted sympathetically, and little Can Opener burst into tears. Everybody liked Kettle. She had lived in the kitchen longer than any of them.

"What shall we do, Kettle?" asked Teapot anxiously. "There must be something. The kitchen won't be the same without you."

Kettle gave a sigh. "Nothing," she said sadly. "It's true. I'm getting old now. All those years of boiling water have worn me out." A little tear fell from her eye and trickled down her side.

"Rubbish," said Freezer. "We're not just going to sit back and let an old friend be thrown out. Besides, those new electric kettles are terribly stuck up.

"I think we should go on strike," said Stove. "I'll refuse to work when they turn me on tomorrow."

"Good idea!" agreed Freezer. "In fact, I think I'll turn myself off now. Then all my food will have spoiled by the morning."

"I'll make my door stick, so they can't put the clothes in," decided Washing Machine.

"I'll bite the woman's finger when she opens the cat food," promised Can Opener, cheering up at the thought.

"I shan't mix the food," declared Food Mixer.

"And I shall refuse to grind the beans," added Coffee Grinder.

"If one of those snobbish new kettles tries pouring boiling water into me, I shall jump on to the floor and break into a thousand pieces," wept Teapot. "We belong together, Kettle."

"Thank you, friends," said Kettle with a sigh.

The next morning, the Brand family was surprised to find that nothing in the kitchen worked properly! Stove remained cold, Freezer had defrosted himself, Washing Machine's door was stuck, Food Mixer refused to scramble eggs, and Coffee Grinder wouldn't whizz around. Even Can Opener cut Mrs. Brand's finger when she tried to open a can of cat food.

"Whatever's happening?" said Mrs. Brand.

"It must be something to do with the electricity," said Mr. Brand. "Let's make a fire, and we'll put the kettle on that. At least we can have a cup of tea."

And that's just what they did.

"It's lucky we didn't throw the kettle out yesterday," said Mr. Brand, sipping his tea.

"Yes it is," agreed Mrs. Brand. "Actually, I'm rather fond of that old kettle, you know. It belonged to my mother. It's getting too old to boil water in, but I think I'd like to keep it after all. I shall fill it with flowers and put it on the counter."

And that's what happened. Kettle was polished up, filled with flowers and put in pride of place on the counter. It suited her perfectly. Holding flowers was much easier for her than boiling water.

Soon, the new kettle arrived to take over her duties. She wasn't at all stuck up, and Kettle was able to give her lots of useful advice.

85

Bradley Bear
Builds a Raft

"Come on, Bradley!" called Jenny and Jimmy, one hot day. "We're going to the river to make a raft!"

"Lovely," thought Bradley. "It's cool on the river."

"There's lots to carry," said Jimmy, pointing to the big pile of planks, ropes, hammers, nails and long poles.

"I'll help," thought Bradley. "I'm good like that."

"I'm carrying my sailing hat," explained Jimmy. "It's quite heavy."

"And I'm carrying the flag, because it's important," said Jenny, waving her handkerchief. "You can bring the rest, Bradley." And off they ran.

"Typical," sighed Bradley, staring at the huge pile.

Picking everything up wasn't easy for Bradley. Something always went wrong. Something always dropped. Finally, by cleverly balancing the planks on his head, he managed it.

"Hurry up," said Jimmy, as Bradley came puffing up. "We've been waiting for **ages**. First, we'll nail the planks together. Pass the hammer, please."

Nailing the planks together was hard. Those planks just didn't want to be nailed. Jimmy kept missing and hammering his thumb.

"Let's rope them together," suggested Jenny.

Roping the planks together was hard. That rope had a mind of its own. It knotted itself up. It got into tangles. It tripped everyone up.

"I'm tired of this," said Jenny crossly. "It's too hot to make a raft. Come on, Jimmy, let's go and play."

"What, give up?" thought Bradley. "Just like that? After carrying everything all this way? Not me. I'll make the raft by myself, and surprise them." And he set to work.

It was a strange raft that Bradley made. **Very** strange indeed.

"Now," thought Bradley. "I'll put it to the test. If the raft floats, it won't matter if it looks funny."

He pushed it into the water. It floated. Sort of. Carefully, Bradley stepped on. Still it floated. Sort of. Bradley picked up the pole and bravely pushed off. The raft wobbled across the water.

"Oh dear," thought Bradley. "My feet are getting wet."

The raft began to spin as well as wobble. Bradley felt quite dizzy. "Goodness," he thought. "Now my knees are wet! I don't think this raft is floating any more. Not even sort of."

He was right. The raft was sinking. Bradley jammed the pole down into the river bed and clung on. Slowly, the raft vanished below the surface. Slowly, Bradley went with it. He slipped lower down the pole . . and lower . .

"Hey! Look at Bradley!" shouted Jimmy from the bank. "He's climbing up the pole!"

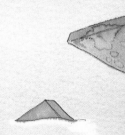

"No he's not," thought Bradley. "He's slipping down it. Help!"

SPLASH! Bradley was in the river. "Well, at least I'm cool now," he thought, as he rose to the surface.

"Wait there, Bradley!" yelled Jenny. "We're coming to join you!"

It was great fun in the water. They raced from the bank to the pole and back again. They climbed up it and slid down it.

"Swimming's better than raft making," said Jimmy, "especially with a pole. How did you manage to get it out here, Bradley?"

"Hmm," thought Bradley. "That would be telling."

Baby Bacon's
Bad Head Cold

Baby Bacon had a bad head cold, which meant that she sneezed a lot. Not only that. She always sneezed at the worst possible times. And when she sneezed, she giggled.

Bobby Bacon built a tower of bricks. It was the highest tower he had ever made, and Bobby felt very pleased with himself.

"ACHOOO!" Baby Bacon sneezed, and the tower came crashing down.

"Bother!" said Bobby.

But Baby Bacon just giggled.

Mrs. Bacon arranged a beautiful vase of flowers, because she was expecting a visitor.

"ACHOOO!" Baby Bacon sneezed the petals off the flowers, leaving a vase of beautifully arranged bare stems.

"Bother!" said Mrs. Bacon.

But Baby Bacon just giggled.

Mr. Bacon liked a cup of hot, frothy coffee in the afternoon. He sat down with it, and Baby Bacon sneezed. She sneezed the froth all over Mr. Bacon's clean shirt.

"Bother!" said Mr. Bacon.

But Baby Bacon just giggled.

Baby Bacon sneezed the stamps out of Grandad Bacon's stamp album, and the pom-poms off Grandma Bacon's slippers. Each time, she giggled.

"That baby's got a head cold," said Mrs. Bacon. "I must get her some special medicine." And she did.

Baby Bacon stopped sneezing. But head colds are catching. The next day, everyone else had one.

Bobby Bacon really didn't mean to sneeze Baby Bacon's teddy bear out of the window.

Baby Bacon didn't giggle. She cried.

"That's the trouble with babies," said Bobby to his mother. "They've got a funny sense of humor."

Little Red Riding Hood

(Traditional tale)

Once upon a time, there was a little girl who lived with her mother in a house on the edge of a wood. She had a bright red cloak with a hood, and so she was often called Little Red Riding Hood.

One morning, her mother asked her to take a basket of good things to her grandmother, who was ill.

Red Riding Hood set off proudly with the basket. Granny's cottage lay through the woods, which were full of flowers.

"I'll pick some flowers for Granny," she thought.

Suddenly, from out of the dark trees, there came a wolf! He had great big ears, great big eyes, and great big pointy teeth!

"Good morning, child," said the wolf. "Where are

you going this fine morning?"

"I'm going to visit Granny," explained Red Riding Hood. "She's ill."

"How kind," said the wolf. "And where does Granny live?"

"About a mile away, in a little thatched cottage close by a stream."

"Well," said the wolf. "Enjoy your walk. And don't talk to strangers. I must be off to get my breakfast," and he vanished into the trees.

The wolf hurried as fast as he could until he reached Granny's cottage. He knocked on the door – one, two, three!

"Who's there?" called Granny.

"Little Red Riding Hood," replied the wolf in a high voice. Wasn't he wicked?

Poor Granny was a bit deaf, otherwise she would have known it wasn't her granddaughter's voice. "Lift up

the latch, dear, and come in," she said.

In rushed the wolf. He jumped on the bed, and swallowed Granny up in a single mouthful. Then, he dressed himself in her night clothes, climbed into bed and waited.

At last, he heard Red Riding Hood come skipping up the path. Tap, tap, tap, went Red Riding Hood on the door.

"Who's there?" called the wolf, imitating Granny's voice.

"Little Red Riding Hood."

"Lift up the latch, dear, and come in," called the wicked wolf.

In came Red Riding Hood. It was dark inside the little cottage, and she felt rather frightened. Somehow, Granny didn't look quite the same as usual.

"Oh Granny," she said. "What big eyes you have!"

"All the better to see you with," replied the wolf.

"But Granny! What big ears you have!"

"All the better to hear you with," said the wolf.

"Granny! What big teeth you have!" quavered Red Riding Hood.

"All the better to eat you with!" howled the wolf, and he sprang out of bed and seized Little Red Riding Hood by her cloak, meaning to eat her up.

As luck would have it, a woodcutter was at work nearby. Hearing Red Riding Hood scream, he rushed in and killed that wicked wolf with one stroke of his ax! Quickly, he cut the wolf open and out stepped Granny, alive and well.

Little Red Riding Hood and her grandmother were, of course, very grateful to the woodcutter, and he was glad he had been able to save them both. They all shared the basket of good things, and then it was time for Little Red Riding Hood to go home. The woodcutter kindly walked all the way home with her to make sure she was quite safe, and Little Red Riding Hood promised not to talk to strangers in the wood again.